THE DIRTIEST TOILET HUMOR BOOK EVER

THE DIRTIEST TOILET HUMOR BOOK EVER

Michael Ryan

iUniverse, Inc.
New York Lincoln Shanghai

The Dirtiest Toilet Humor Book Ever

iUniverse, Inc.

For information address:
iUniverse, Inc.
2021 Pine Lake Road, Suite 100
Lincoln, NE 68512
www.iuniverse.com

ISBN: 0-595-31173-3

Printed in the United States of America

Contents

INTRODUCTION

2 %

What is the significance of this number? Well, to many people, myself included, it means a huge deal. Let me explain. I spend around an average of 30 minutes on the toilet a day. I usually take three to four dumps a day at around eight minutes each. So these 30 minutes spent crapping out of the total 1440 minutes per day (24 hours x 60 min.) is 30/1440 or approximately 2%. So I spend 2 % of my day shitting. If I live to 100, that would mean I spent a whole two years taking shits. Two years! For the mathematically challenged, if I lived to 50, that's a year spent on the can. Anyway you look at it, if you are a normal male; a great portion of your life is in the bathroom.

Crapping is rarely spoken of despite the fact it is a daily ritual. Yes, the majority considers it a vulgar topic. It is smelly, messy and disgusting. But, at the same time, it is a natural function and we have to live with it. Everyone knows about it, so why not talk about it? In fact, you have probably experienced or heard of all these things about to be mentioned in this book, yet never discussed any of them. Yes, it may be true I am a little disturbed and enjoy this topic more than most. But beneath everyone's outer shell, there lies a little place that wants to burst out laughing about the topic of SHITTING. So let down your guard a little and enjoy it.

TYPES OF SHIT

Let's jump right into it. I am sure you have heard the saying that no two snowflakes are alike. Well, I don't believe it. When it snows, billions of snowflakes fall to the ground. They are so tiny making it rather difficult to accept such a theory. Plus is there a guy who catches these snowflakes mid-air and studies their composition before they melt or combine with other snowflakes? However I do believe that no two shits are alike. Before I flush I always stare in awe at the fruits of my labor. Of the infinite varieties, there are a few deserving recognition.

1. The Freebie. This is my personal favorite. The odds in Vegas have this one at 60-1. It comes only once every two months. This is a bowel movement that gives the lazy, fat man an orgasm. After dumping, the first wipe of the ass shows nothing. Clean as a whistle. In disbelief, you wipe again, thinking you must have missed. Again, there is nothing. It's like winning the lottery. Pull up your pants and get on with your lucky day.

2. The Shocker. This type has been known to give older people heart attacks. Each time the shocker occurs, I cringe. When the doody ball drops from the butthole, it falls six inches before hitting the water. It's like a little kid doing a cannon ball off the diving board, soaking everyone around him. Well, same with this shit. The cold water splashes you right where you don't want it. You jump up in shock and wish you had prepared for it. Maybe next time in anticipation, you will jump up before contact.

3. The One Footer. No, not a sub sandwich. This is the one where you purposely forget to flush so others can share it. The shit never breaks when coming out. It curls around like a rattlesnake. If you don't feel better after this one, you got problems.

4. Corn on the Cob. What a great one! This is fun for all ages, especially the males. So you had corn for dinner last night? You take a dump, look at it, and marvel at the little pieces perfectly intact. Does anyone ever digest corn? I don't understand. I feel if I eat 100 pieces of canned corn, I'll see those 100 the next day. Well anyway, to add to the experience, anticipate this dump and save your piss. Afterwards, stand up and piss on the corn. Watch them pop like popcorn kernels. You are now starring in a live video game.

5. Mexican Night. This one can lead to a panic. I first mistook this one as a symptom of dying. The contents in the toilet were entirely red. It looked like a gallon of blood. Then I remembered the salsa and chips, tacos, burritos, beans and whatever else I had eaten. That's scary shit.

6. The Mile High. For some this may happen often while for others almost or always never. In order to do this, you need two huge meals, maybe three, before you dispose of your waste products. This dump earns its name because the pile rises above the water level line. This is when your shit really stinks. It is the part of the iceberg you see above the water that lets out that telltale aroma.

7. The What the Hell is that Shit? This is a mixture of everything that you thought would never come out of your body. There are some standard logs, some liquid shit, some floaters, some flower-like turds and every other new shape you never knew existed. This is as abstract as the art of shitting can get. Try taking a picture and submitting it to a gallery.

8. The Perfect Poo. For a slob like myself, I have never experienced this one. Most normal people have, or so I am told. So bear with me, as the following is second-hand information. This one is made up of three to four doody logs, all perfectly uniform in length and width. The delivery is as smooth as butter. The wipe requires the textbook 3.5 swipes. The time it takes is only two minutes. Supposedly it tickles your ass as it gently and graciously slides out. It falls ever so gently into the water and does not even make a splash.

9. The Splasher. Do this one at your own home, pig. This unique poo-poo is accompanied by diarrhea, a whole chapter I cover later. After this one, all sides of the toilet are painted with remains of your last meal. We're talking smoth-ered in shit. The decoration remains for quite some time. So feel proud, you left an impression.

10. The Screamer. This one comes in two versions. It can occur while in the throes of diarrhea or constipation. Either way it is not fun. The burning sensa-tion with rhea (short for diarrhea) is comparable to sticking your hand in a fire. Your precious bunghole just can't take it. After taking seven dumps already that day and wiping after each one, your little hole is worn out. Don't

be afraid to scream. The other moment of terror is while being constipated. This one is like giving birth to a 13-pound baby…. through your ass. You think to yourself, "Why me?" This sucks! It just plain sucks!

11. The Double Flusher. This one still gives me the chills. It brings a sense of satisfaction and accomplishment. After its completion, I feel like a real man. As the name suggests, this hefty load requires multiple flushes. You're putting your toilet into overdrive. A little embarrassing if you're at your girlfriend's or in-laws and they hear the flushes. But who cares? Pat yourself on the shoulder and leave the bathroom with a smile for a job well done.

12. R.E.M. No, this is not the band, but the stage in sleep where your dreams occur. This one is particularly heinous and I wouldn't wish it on my worst enemy. You are sound asleep, dreaming about a threesome with a couple of Florida State cheerleaders, when you realize you have to take a shit. Myth: If you go back to sleep it will go away. Don't kid yourself. If it woke you up, it has to get out. So you crawl out of bed searching for the light switch, while stubbing your toe and banging into walls and doors. A few bruises and cuts later, you make it to the bathroom. Always check and make sure the seat is down. I would rather be kicked in the balls than sit down with the seat up. Be careful not to fall asleep while sitting on the can, it is very tempting. This dump is rough because there is nothing else to do. You're too tired to read, plus there's no chance you would turn the light on and blind yourself, so you just have to grunt and bear it.

13. The Your Life Sucks Dump. This one can ruin a day. While sitting preparing to dump, you simultaneously take a piss. Your concentration is off or you may have a boner (you have some problems) and you proceed to piss through the little crack in between the seat and the toilet base. Of course this gets all over your pants. If you're at work or on a date, you're screwed. Always aim your penis downwards. Always.

LOCATION

Where the shit is taken is extremely important. There is nothing better than the home court advantage that your own toilet offers. You feel so at ease. However, when playing away games the opposing arenas completely suck. Here are some of the worst.

1. Girlfriend's House. What good can come out of this? You lose either way. I find it impossible to unload if the toilet is anywhere within a 15-foot radius of her or her family. What if I rip a loud fart? Walls are only so thick. Also, the longer I take the grosser she thinks I am. I hate it. One situation, which I hope you never encounter, is the fake versus real fart game. Let me explain. I was stuck in a small hostel in Europe at night and had to shit. The room was a bed and a bathroom right on top of each other. I had to shit and there was nowhere for my girlfriend to go. I had to go in the bathroom while she lay on the bed. There was no radio to block out the sound from the explosion I knew would follow. The sink (which I usually turn on full blast to help tone out my gas) had absolutely no pressure, just dripped water. I had to improvise. I started making fart noises with my mouth. She started laughing while probably crying in the inside. She knew they were fake ones. Of course I am mixing in some real ones with the fake ones. She starts catching on and yelling "fake" or "real" with each one. This definitely took some pressure off me and let me complete my business. She is a keeper.

2. The Gas Station. This one I just do not understand. You have to ask for a key first from the attendant. So you think this bathroom will be nice and clean. It's the complete opposite. It's a shit hole. The 3' x 3' room is barely lit. If you are lucky you need to only wipe off the piss on the seat from the last asshole. Then you have to put at least three layers of toilet paper on the seat. Don't touch anything! Think of how many slobs have shat (past tense of shit) in

there. You do not have to worry about washing your hands. If for some reason the sink should work, it's an almost guarantee there won't be any soap. But you can't blame the gas station attendant. If I were him, I would never go in there either.

3. The Library. This one is entertaining. You get the choice of five stalls from which to choose. On the walls are slogans that you can never forget, such as, "Confucius says man who eats many prunes, sits on toilet many moons" and "Here I sit broken hearted, tried to shit but only farted." Then there are the quotes that scare me such as, "Be here March 15th at 8pm for hot, anal sex." I always kick myself for not sending a pledge in my fraternity house there at this time.

4. The Outhouse. This is always a last resort. There's no flush. Do not attempt to breathe once inside. Do not touch anything. Layer the seat with toilet paper for five minutes straight. Forget that, just squat. Everything about this experience gives me the chills. Avoid this at all costs.

5. The Airplane. This is one of the wonders of the world. Where does your crap go? I have heard that it is let out of the plane while in flight. Can't be true, I hope. The bathroom is really small and uncomfortable. Once you pick your position for shitting, there's no room to move. So think first. I feel so bad for fat people on the plane. How the hell do they do that? Here is one quick story. On a flight to Florida with my family, my brother disrupted the life of 200 or so people. He was taking a shit on the plane when we were about to land. The pilot made an announcement that we were going to land and asked everyone to return to his or her seat. My brother did not come out. The flight attendants had to knock on the door several times, but he kept saying, "One minute." The pilot had to enter a holding pattern and circle the plane around waiting for him to come out. As he left the bathroom, everyone applauded. This was truly an unforgettable moment in shitting for him. His face was red as a tomato. This scarred him for life. So make sure if you do take a shit, do it early on in the flight.

6. Restaurant. Most of the time these are clean as a whistle. But remember the rule of thumb, cheap restaurant, scummy bathroom. This bowel movement is sometimes a rushed one. A lot of the bathrooms have only one shitter. While shitting, at least for me, several people walk in and pull on the door to find it locked. Sometimes, they wait there near the sink. I see them through the crack where the door meets the stall. This pisses me off. I do not need any additional pressure. Most of the time, they'll come back after a few minutes to find the door locked again. Again, this pisses me off. Go shit somewhere else.

Leave me alone. Hey, if you want, I'll come and get you at your table when I am done. Oddly, it seems everyone gets real quiet in the bathroom. There is not much dialogue. I am surprised I have never heard anyone exclaim, "How much longer 'til you finish?" That would definitely throw my dumping game off.

7. Office Building. I love the elevator music! It is very relaxing. Also, you'll never see a stall without toilet paper. So far, so good. But then I am confronted by my worst enemy, the automatic flush sensor. Maybe it's just me, but this thing goes off every time I move. If I sneeze, it goes off. I don't mind the clean, new water but I hate the splash. Even worse is when I am making the nest on the seat before I sit. When I go to sit down, it flushes soaking the toilet paper I just so neatly placed. Then I have to do it again. This reoccurring cycle goes on and on.

8. Outdoors. You gotta do it once in your life. You will be one with nature. Personally, I have done it four times. The first time was while hiking in the High Uinta Mountains in Utah. I was on a teen tour, which is 12 spoiled teenagers who travel with two guides out West. I was backpacking there for seven days. I grabbed the roll of paper and went off on my own. Finally, finding the perfect spot, I dug a little hole. I squatted and shat. What an experience! It took a while and was a little uncomfortable. It was difficult to keep my balance. Plus, the gathering flies didn't help. I was just happy I did not live in India where this practice is common. Sadly, less than half of the people in India have toilets in their homes. Getting back to the story, the guides told us to keep our used toilet paper in a brown paper bag and put it in our backpacks because it is bad for the environment. Hell no! Sorry nature, but I am leaving everything.

A different experience, though truly incredible, took place in Arizona. There was some company that rented out circular inflatable tubes that you could take down a river. This ordeal was boring as well as time consuming. The current was barely existent and the experience was lame altogether until I felt that urge. I had to drop a bomb! What the hell was I going to do? So I pulled down my bathing suit, lying on my back, with my ass in the water, and shat. It felt awesome. Sucked however for the people coming down from behind me.

9. The Camp Experience. For those of you who went to overnight camp or who have children that did or will, this one is a guarantee. Most likely you're in the middle of the woods. For me it was in Lake Delton, Wisconsin. Numerous times I took shits in a stall with the company of a couple of frogs, daddy long-leg spiders and some moths the size of birds. Too much time was spent making sure one of those creatures didn't touch me.

10. The Fraternity. This one is just not fun. I lived in a frat house for two and a half years and encountered this one too many times. There's never toilet paper. There's probably puke on the floor and there's definitely piss on the seat. Half of the time you open the stall door and see the toilet clogged and overflowing.

11. Eastern Europe. I am taking a dump in Austria when I notice a stench that could have killed a baby cow. I am looking around me to see where the odor is coming from, when I recall there's only one stall in the bathroom. Ten minutes later, woozy and confused, I get up to wipe and look at my artwork. I quickly realize the source of the foul aroma. The toilet is set up in way that breeds nastiness. The front of the toilet bowl has a hole and the backside slopes upward putting it a good six inches above the hole where there is no toilet water. So I have a pile of manure sitting on this "second level." This shit is just sitting there. There is no water for my turds to swim in. Of course it stinks! Man is this country backwards. I flush the toilet just before passing out and then a tidal wave of water comes forth from the back of the toilet pushing my crap to the hole at the front. I would like to meet the genius engineer who invented this toilet.

12. Somewhere in Mexico. So I am in the middle of a no-name town in Mexico when we approach a restaurant/market area. There in the middle of this area is a bathroom surrounded by mean looking fat ladies sitting on chairs. They are guarding the bathroom like it is a secret vault holding billions of dollars. In reality, they are working there collecting money for an act I strongly oppose charging for. Why would I pay to take a piss or even a shit when I could do it outside for free? Fortunately for them, I didn't have to do either. To make matters even worse, there was an additional charge for extra toilet paper. You only get a few squares of toilet paper. I wipe a lot. I want a clean butthole. I need 15-20 squares for that. It would have cost me about $5 to shit here, which was more than my meal cost.

13. Monte Carlo, France. Go there. If nothing else, go to take a shit. Here they treat your ass like royalty. I took a dump in a public bathroom that had marble floors and walls. I walked toward the stall and heard a noise. It sounded like a spray can. I opened the stall door and the noise stopped. This noise was an automatic, sensor controlled air-purifying system. It smelled like roses. It stops spraying when you enter. I take a seat on the biggest toilet I have ever seen. There is no possible way for my pecker to touch the front of the seat, which is truly the grossest thing in the world. I finish, get up and flush when I realize this robot for a toilet is run by a computer-like system. There is a box

above the toilet with French words followed by little lights. The first light went on and the toilet seat rotated while a mechanism popped out and disinfected the seat. Then it was rinsed. Then it was dried. This was truly a miracle. When I finally left the toilet, after flushing and watching this truly ingenious invention a few more times, I heard the spray kick in. I went back a few hours later, not even having to shit. I just wanted to see it one more time before I left. I sat there like a kid in a candy store.

14. The Uffizi in Florence, Italy. I wait in line for two hours to go to this museum and of course I have to take a shit right away. So I run to the bathroom to find an open stall waiting for me. I go in to find a toilet with no seat. In fact, none of the toilets had seats. Was this a joke? Do museum people not shit? I didn't understand nor had time to think of a plan. So I squatted and shat my brains out. For this inconvenience I pissed all over the floor.

THE WALK

You can spot the dude who has to pinch a loaf a mile away if you know what to look for. This poor, pathetic person is walking extremely slow, pausing occasionally, and trying to keep his butt cheeks closed together. You may ask why I feel bad for this person? Well, this guy is usually me. My intestines have no patience. When I have to go, I have to go. I am stuck doing this dance until I find a toilet. Chances are I have a little turtlehead coming out. I have to think about not shitting in order to hold it in. I once used my finger as a butt plug to push the turtlehead back in. I cannot have a conversation of any sort at this time or I will lose my focus and shit all over myself. I have come perilously close on occasion and unfortunately believe one day this will happen. So next time you see someone walking this way, move aside and leave him alone.

SHITTING ATTIRE

This is your time, baby. Enjoy it! Remember, you are free from all your worries and stresses. So be like most avid shitters and get naked. I rip my shirt off and put on my game face. I like to do this regardless of where I shit. Call me crazy, but it makes me feel like one with the toilet. I do keep my pants on, well, at my ankles. Some of my friends rip those off too. That's a little too much for me. What happens when that spider, monster, or the thing you dreaded coming out of the toilet when you are shitting, does indeed make an appearance? You can't run out of the bathroom naked, but shirt off is okay. See, you have to think.

THE SEAT

This is a very important part of the process. The comfortableness of the seat is an individual preference. Some people like a porcelain, hard seat. I personally do not. It is too hard and cold. If I sit for a while, my butt hurts. If I am sweaty, I slip all over. I prefer a cushiony, soft seat. It's utopia for my ass. My ass sinks in and the seat conforms to my shape. I sit for a hell of a lot longer when ensconced on one of these seats. There's also the fur-covered seat. This is a sexy thing in an area that has nothing sexy about it.

Regardless of the seat, the worst part is when the tip of your penis hits the front end of the seat. I feel violated and contaminated. Who else's dirty shlong has hit that part of the seat? So for this reason I have fallen in love with the incomplete oval seats. You know, the ones with a space in the middle like the letter "U." This is where it's at. You can let go of your wiener without the fear of getting gonorrhea.

Finally, I have the compulsion to cover up any seat, outside of my own, when shitting. I hate the thought of my bare ass touching the same spot where a fat, sweaty scumbag's ass has touched. It adds a few minutes to the dumping experience but it creates a real sense of security.

One last thought for you to ponder. Why is there sometimes shit on the seat? Don't people know how to shit? Aren't they aware of where their asshole is located?

THE IDEAL STALL

As previously discussed there will be times when you have to shit in a public bathroom. This sucks! Yet, when your turds are knocking at the door, you have to open it and let 'em out. An ideal stall at a public place is at least four and a half feet wide. The floors are glistening, with no piss on them. On the backside of the stall door is a coat hanger. I'd rather die than put my jacket or bag on the floor. The seat should be sparkling clean with plenty of toilet paper left in the dispenser. Above you, hanging from the ceiling is a television playing sports non-stop. There should be newspapers, *Playboy* and *Maxim* available on a shelf next to you. While we are at it, there should be a hot chick (who can't smell or hear) behind you giving you a nice massage.

TOILET PAPER

When it comes to home items, this is an area that I do not mess with. I am cheap and I can't help it. I love generic products. However, I hate a stingy person who buys 1-ply. This is an insult. This may be the worst invention of all time. What the hell is the point of it? It is torture. Single ply always rips, sending my finger up into the hole of messiness. Once the finger is up there it takes forever to get it clean. You have to wash it over and over again to rid the smell. When I come across this, I solve the problem by just folding it over, making it 2-ply. Get back at that cheap, inhospitable sorry excuse for a person and don't flush.

I love those rich people with the scented toilet paper. It's a guarantee that it's 2-ply and it smells good. Then there are the extra soft brands. That stuff feels so good, I sometime just wipe for the fun of it.

Of course, there are the times when there is no toilet paper. You have to resort to Kleenex or worse case scenario, paper towels. Don't be deceived by the soft, lotion Kleenex. Yeah, it feels great but the aftermath is not worth it. You get itchy asshole. Kleenex is not meant for the butthole. You spend the rest of the day scratching your ass and moving your butt back and forth on your chair to rid the itch. Now if you use paper towels, remember two sheets per flush. Anymore and you'll clog the sucker up. In college a couple of times I was so desperate I had to use computer paper. This was awful giving me paper cuts and leaving a lot of shit left to be wiped (which I realized later).

Finally, they're coming out or already have with wet wipes for adults. These new wipes are meant for the baby boomers as they are reaching old age. Old people (not all) have a tougher time wiping and to be quite honest sometimes smell like shit. They don't have the energy for a full, complete wiping.

PUBIC HAIR

How does this fit in you may wonder? Not a main ingredient in the process, but an external variable that can make or break a shit. Almost every toilet seat has a pubic hair on it. Whose is it? Where is it? To answer the first question, if it's yours, no big deal. Chances are it is not. One quick swipe with toilet paper in hand, it's gone. Yet, a pain to see and think about. Location wise, if it's near the front of the seat, it's definitely a pube. Near the back part, possible ass hair. They are both gross. The worst is when you are at your grandparent's house and there are the gray pubes.

TEMPERATURE

A small factor, yet makes a huge contribution to successful crapping is the climate. Everything has to be just perfect. Therefore the temperature must be comfortable, not being too hot or too cold. When it's too cold, goose bumps develop and the turds get stuck. They don't want to come out when it's like the South Pole. Can't blame them.

When it's too hot, forget about enjoyment. We're talking pure struggle. You're fighting beads of sweat dripping down, a seat covered with moisture and thoughts of fainting. Why don't you just kick me in the nuts? It's the same thing. So if you have no central air conditioning, buy a fan so shit takers in your house don't have to suffer through this agony.

GRUNTING

Is it really necessary? I personally hate those meatheads in the weight room who scream out loud on lifts. These bastards do it for attention. It's like saying, "Hey everyone look at me. I am lifting heavy weights." In this arena it may have a different meaning. We have all had the experience of sitting next to someone in a stall that is grunting. I feel bad for this guy while at the same time disliking him for distracting me in my process. Clench your fists together or something.

If you are by yourself, then belt it out. I have done this on emergency I-am-going-to-shit-in-my-pants diarrhea. Why deny this opportunity for enjoyment? Next time you are having a great orgasm, try not to make a sound. It's tough. So if you have thick walls, just don't care or are by yourself go with the grunt. It may make you feel manly.

BATHROOM SPRAY

Air freshener is my personal savior. I cannot even express how many times I have stunk up a bathroom at a friend's house. This invention is essential for the dreaded dump at my girlfriend's house.

Now for the negatives. This stuff stinks. Each time I spray it, I somehow manage to inhale it through my mouth, leading me to gag. I use the spray and run technique. This involves spraying while your feet are out of the room, then dropping the spray can and getting the hell out of there. Also, whenever I walk into a bathroom that was just sprayed (not including Monte Carlo), I want to throw up. It's like your own fart. You don't mind your own gas, even though it stinks, but you hate everyone else's gas. I hate when anyone else sprays the bathroom.

Yes, the trade-off is worth it. I'd rather inhale the air freshener than my father's smelly shit. Yet, it's a lose-lose situation. For the bathrooms that don't have this, I feel bad for the owner(s). Why not spend the extra few bucks so you don't have to fumigate the sacred room?

Another option is the plug in. This feature keeps the room smelling good all the time. This is clearly the best choice. I would love to smell wild flowers before I walk in the room, while shitting and upon leaving the bathroom.

HYGIENE

After I finish my business, I feel it's necessary to cleanse my hands. So you are thinking, big deal, so do all normal people. However, some bathrooms are not equipped for this. There is one and only one way to wash your hands after shitting, liquid soap. If I am at a restaurant or at a friend's house and there is a bar of soap, I refuse to use it. It's simply disgusting. Why would I want to rub my hands on a bar where someone prior to me rubbed their doody-stained hands? So cough up the extra few bucks and have some dignity. Think of it this way. Would you want your guests walking around your house, grabbing your food with their dirty hands?

The worst was in my fraternity house. There was no soap. So after every crap, my fraternity brothers would rinse their hands under the faucet, using only the water. Later, these guys would go the dining room and touch all the food. I had to eat this food.

The worst experience I ever had was when I walked into the frat house cook's bathroom. This little shack of a bathroom, in the back of the kitchen, had a bar of soap lying on the sink. It looked drier than a desert, with a pubic hair smothered into it. It looked as if it hadn't been used for weeks. That left me with a good feeling. So please, if the opportunity presents itself, wash your hands. I hate having to think if a person's hand I shook was clean.

There's one more area applicable to this hygiene chapter. I need to dry my hands after washing them. The hot air blow dryer is fantastic. I love hitting the silver button. The paper towel dispenser is sufficient as well. What is better than finishing a dump and being given the opportunity to toss your paper towel in the garbage and either score or miss (and not caring at all because it's not your house)? However, the revolving cloth that some public bathrooms have is completely ridiculous. Who in their right mind would use it? What's the point of washing your hands, if you are going to use that bacteria infested, should-be-obsolete, doody-stained, piss-stained, nasty, reused cloth?

PORTA POTTY

These miniature toilets are made for little children before they are old enough for a real size toilet. These mini-toilets are so cute. I wish I had an adult-sized one now. How convenient is this device? They should make inexpensive fold up porta potties available for all sizes. Perfect for road trips. Instead of having to zombie walk to the bathroom in the middle of the night, you could just plop down on your porta potty next to your bed.

FLUSHES

1. Courtesy Flush. I am not the biggest fan of this. Hey, if you could stink up a whole floor of a house, then you deserve to keep your dump until you're completely finished. There is no such thing as being unable to tolerate the smell of your own crap. However the courtesy flush, asked by my mom hundreds of times when I was younger, is a nice act. Yet, the courage it takes for someone to ask it is usually lacking. So take it upon yourself if you want to do this.

2. The Swirl. So yeah, you've all heard that the toilet flushes in the other direction in the Southern Hemisphere. I thought so too until my adventure to Australia. I went there to see this so-called phenomenon. Upon arrival to the land down under I immediately squeezed out a turd. Everything I had known up until this point (in regards to the clock-wise flush) would be opposite. Well, I got screwed. Utterly confused and disappointed, the flush had no swirl whatsoever. It was a complete suction movement downwards. Got right back on the plane and came home.

3. Mr. Efficiency. This is a poor excuse for a toilet. Two buttons in some cases control the flush. One button is for a half flush, for such things as urination or a baby dump. Fortunately, these choices are present on only a few public toilets. As far as the half flushes, who pisses in a stall when there are urinals? It is only those guys who are ashamed of their manhood. That's a whole other story. Eh, let me get into it. I hate you guys that piss in the toilets when there are urinals available. You pigs piss all over the seat and ruin it for the unfortunate one that comes in next, usually me, who has to shit. Sorry, so back to the efficiency things. I tried to test my dump with a half flusher and I felt the toilet give me a look like I was crazy. It may have sucked down a fifth. I did it a few more times and finally after four flushes, it was gone. Now how are four 1/2 flushes more efficient than one full flush?

There are also these new one-gallon tanks that only have energy efficient flushes. You're stuck flushing multiple times each dump. The first flush is just for the shit. Then every two wipes require an additional flush. This is ridiculous. More then two-thirds of our planet is covered by water. Why do we need to conserve it? If anything, we need less water and more land. If I am ever at a guest's house that has one of these flushers (with no option but the energy efficient) I will leave them a nice surprise, my shit clogged in the toilet. I am not going to waste my time flushing for an hour.

THE FAN

No you usually don't have a crowd of people cheering you on when you shit. I am talking about that noise that comes on sometimes when you turn on the light. This is great, sometimes. It should always be optional. There should be a switch for the fan and a separate one for the light. Why would I want the noisy fan going when I am by myself in my home? This throws off my utopian setting.

Nevertheless, it is extremely helpful. Not only does it help with the smell, let me say marginally though, but also it hides your noises. This friend you never realized you had blocks out most of your grunts and farts you don't want anyone outside the bathroom to hear. So take advantage and let 'em rip.

THE NEIGHBOR

Every now and then you're at some public place (i.e., a restaurant) and there is someone in the stall next to you. Some people are embarrassed by this situation. There's no reason to be. I have encountered numerous weird neighbors. I have heard the moans, the loud farts and the diarrhea. Why not live it up and have some fun? Make some extra loud groans and fake cries. The loud grunt gets the whole bathroom quiet. Pound your foot on the ground and hit the stall for added attention.

Now the best situation for me is when I am shitting with a friend in the next stall. To a man this is a true bond. It's sharing an intimate, macho experience. I love conversing back and forth. Then there are the practical jokes. I have done this sick one plenty of times. While wiping I raise a piece of doody-stained paper over the stall so my friend can see it. In my other hand is a clean piece of toilet paper. I say, "Hey, see this? Catch." Of course I throw the clean one over but it is guaranteed to freak him out.

THE BIDET

Hands down, the best invention. The inventor deserves a Nobel Peace Prize or something. Eliminates 90% of wiping. All you have to do is dry your poop chute. Unfortunately it's very uncommon; with only a few rich friends of mine having it. I had to try it. Felt great! I need one.

Other than its intended use, there are many more creative applications. Use it as a water fountain or brush your teeth with it. Perfect for blowing up water balloons. Someone needs to make these cheaper and install them all over. Everyone would have a smile on his or her face. Depression rates would drop significantly. Forget social security checks; give an old person one of these. After 60 years of wiping, one deserves a bidet.

CLOGGING THE BOWL

Almost everyone in his or her lifetime has clogged a toilet. Personally, I have clogged far too many. No I am not bragging. Half of my clogs are due to the excessive amount of toilet paper I line the seat with and my obsession with a perfectly clean bunghole. The clog ordeal is solved with the plunger. What brainiac invented this tool? It works every time. It should be a law that every bathroom be equipped with one.

There was an incident where this law would have helped my social life. It took place during my freshman year of college. I was sort of dating this girl. Anyway, I stayed over at her place. I woke myself up the next morning with a huge fart. Luckily, I think she did not hear it. The fart was a warning signal for the massive amount of rhea that was on its way. I unloaded four pounds of sloppy manure only to realize that I had clogged her bowl. As you can guess, there was no plunger. I was shit out of luck (no pun intended). I had no idea what to do. So I went back into her room and said I had to leave and go study. I was out of there like a fat girl in dodgeball. This was at 6:00am on Sunday. Most people were just going to bed at this hour. I was hoping she'd think it was one of her roommates. That was the last time she saw me. Oddly, she never returned my phone calls.

Does the overflow really happen? It seems the toilet knows the exact amount of water to add when it is clogged. The level gets so close to the brim that you jump out of the way. At the last second it stops. Despite this, it does overflow on occasion and it really dampens your day. We're talking sewer water and turds everywhere. Hopefully it is not at your house.

Back to the plunger and its rubber end. It is quite possibly the last thing I would ever want to touch. However, a friend once asked me if I would lick a plunger for $1000. I had to say "yes." That is a lot of money. The medicine to cure my new illness will probably cost less.

WHAT THE HELL DO YOU DO?

This is one of my favorite topics and probably one of the most important for novices to this area. Since so much time is spent on the can, why not use your time wisely. If I were smart, I would read up on the market or do some work. However like I vowed during school I would never do homework on the toilet. Why mix business with pleasure? So have fun with this time. You are away from everything including the phone, wife, kids, work, stress, etc. Enjoy this alone time.

I love reading the newspaper. As do most men, I read from the back to the front. I have to start with the sport's section. As a matter of fact my shit time usually lasts as long as it takes me to read the whole sport section. When the Sunday edition comes out my doody time increases drastically.

Magazines are always great as are books. I once read a novel where I read a new chapter with each bowel movement. My dump ended when the chapter ended. When I was younger, I would play Game Boy by Nintendo (a handheld video game system). Those were the days. Too bad I lost that thing.

Oftentimes I find myself talking on the phone while dropping manure. It's a great time to get rid of those annoying phone calls you have to return. Though this activity is great it is not the easiest. If you are talking to a grandparent who can barely hear, then the following won't matter. You have to time your drop offs with the conversation. You can't pinch a loaf while you are talking. Wait to the other person is talking and then cover your mouthpiece. 100% efficient, right? Wrong! My girlfriend has caught me while donating my wastes to the sewer. She'll say, "What was that?" I respond, "Nothing." Then comes the "What are you doing?" I make up some stupid answer. Regardless of my answer she'll say, "Gross, you are disgusting. You're in the bathroom." All I can do is deny it. It's like she already knew the answer but had to make sure I knew that she knew. So lately, during a big drop off, I have been putting the person on hold, (by pressing the flash button) then returning to converse after losing some weight.

If you are talking to a friend who is the same sex, who cares? If I don't tell them I am taking a shit I make sure they soon find out. While a big delivery to the toilet pool or during a gigantic fart, I put the phone right near by. The reaction used to be great however lately my close friends go on with the conversation as if nothing happened. It's as if they are so used to it that they are immune to this while talking to me. It pisses me off. I want a reaction.

Also don't forget spa time. Make yourself more beautiful. Take the time to clean out your breathing pathways. No one can see you, so go ahead and pick your nose. You can even wipe the boogers on the toilet paper. No need to flick them. After the pick, take a glance at your shoes. Is it time to get a new pair? Do they need a shine? Now is the time you are closest to your shoes so take advantage of it.

When I am not prepared for my dump or am too lazy to get the paper in the morning, improvisation takes place. I have spent many mornings reading the back of tampon boxes. Sort of interesting. I have learned every ingredient in hair gel and memorized all the chemicals in deodorant.

When I was real young and in a hurry before school, I would sometimes eat my breakfast in the bathroom. What kind of Mom did I have? That's grosser than gross. That should be punishable by law. Physically speaking, I used to think it didn't make any sense. Why eat while crapping? Didn't it just come out after swallowing it? Yet I still ate my toast on the shitter.

Far and away the best thing I have seen and is a must buy is a putting green for the toilet. The green astroturf-like material goes from your feet to about four feet away and comes with a plastic golf club and balls. When I get older and learn to like golf this will probably be as much fun as having sex.

MASTURBATION

You're probably thinking what is this topic doing in this book? It's not too far off track though. Most of you have read or heard of the quote, "Here I sit and contemplate, should I shit or masturbate?" I have had my share of NRBs (no reason boners) while shitting. But you can't spank when you are dumping. I think it is illegal. It's just unethical.

I have stupidly brought a nude magazine (*Playboy* or *Hustler*) with me before, telling myself I would only read the articles. My willpower is not that strong. As any man knows anything and everything can lead to a woody. So again, I am stuck with a stiffy while shitting. I tell my little guy I'll take care of him after I finish. However, after wiping I lose all intentions of doing anything. It ruins the mood.

I also know there are some of you out there who feel it is okay to masturbate in a public bathroom stall. This is not okay. You are a sick person who needs help. Stay out of my stalls. Stalls are for shitting and shitting only.

TOILET PAPER HOLDER

A small topic but of great importance. The toilet paper holder should be mounted to the wall next to the toilet, preferably to my left because I am a righty. I pull with my left hand and tear with my right. I have seen the holder on the wall behind me, which is completely inefficient. I have also seen it placed directly in front but a good reach away. If you have this at your house, you deserve to have a guest who drips his shit all over your floor while reaching for the paper. Get it right. This is something so easy yet done wrong way too often.

I have also come across a toilet paper holder that when you pulled the paper, music would play. This little gadget was cute at first, playing *Take me out to the Ballgame*, but after wiping for five minutes until my hole was clean I was sick of the song. I broke that stupid, annoying, waste on my eardrums, dumb thing.

Last bit on the toilet paper holder. I find it extremely frustrating when the toilet paper is placed the wrong way in the holder. When I tug on the paper I want the paper coming from the bottom, with the roll moving counter clockwise (when its on your left side). Think about it. The other way, clockwise, wastes time and energy. If the roll is new and thick, when pulling over the top, the paper prematurely rips preventing you from getting your desired length. So don't be an asshole and put the toilet paper on the wrong way.

WIPING

The good old nature vs. nurture topic. Were we genetically driven to stand or sit while wiping or do we learn through our parents? Young children are usually wiped by their parents. At what age it stops, I don't remember, but weren't those the days. I wish someone would wipe my ass every time I took a shit now. Anyway, my parents had me stand up and then they would wipe me. I think that is why to this day I wipe standing up. It may also be an evolutionary thing. Around 2.4 million years ago, the first human species evolved. I don't suppose these guys had toilets back then consequently having to crap outside. Wiping while standing may have developed in order to see deadly animals or savage, enemy tribes.

I have asked many of my male friends and around 60% sit and 40% stand. Despite these stats, standing is the way to go. Only girls sit and wipe. I feel if you have a penis you should never sit and wipe. Why would you, a male, take the chance of having your hand or arm hitting the dirty toilet when reaching between your legs to wipe? While carefully watching out for this, you have to be certain that the dirty toilet paper doesn't come into contact with your pecker on the return from wiping your ass. This should not be like performing brain surgery. Avoid all of this and just stand. You can maneuver your body to reach all areas of the ass to get a good wiping without having to think.

In regards to the wiping, when is enough enough? I often have problems with this. I feel I can wipe my ass four thousand times and I'd still see shit on the paper. My asshole will never be clean without the bidet. It's a catch 22. Do you wipe until your ass bleeds or do you allow a little doody to remain? Yes, I have drawn blood many times from wiping too much. And, yes, I have left a little shit in my ass as well. This subject, I cannot be very helpful on because I am lost as well. I spend so much time wiping and wiping. It kills me.

Ever try wiping with your weak hand? It is very hard to learn and one messy experiment. I tried it a few times but simply hate it. My coordination is off and by the time I finally get it, my shit is dried up and stuck in my crack.

Finally, the toilet paper crumple or fold over issue. The analogy is like giving someone a high-five or shaking his hand. As one gets older, the handshake becomes more appropriate as does the fold over. Previous research has shown slobs crumple. However, I have done both and feel I am not a slob. There is a time and place for everything. Of course when you are in a rush, the crumple is the only option. Beware this can be messy. You may lose track of where your shit is on the paper and get it on you. If you are thinking that you use only one wipe with each crumpled piece, then I could never be you pal. Forget the waste of paper tree-hugger and think money. Toilet paper is not cheap. I use every damn inch of clean white space possible.

Now the fold over. Yeah it is good, but it does require some attention. Don't prematurely stop wiping because you have gone through the same robotic motion five times and assume you are done without first glancing at the toilet paper. I feel like each flat, predictable but efficient wipe is the same in contrast to the dynamic crumple where you never know the texture you'll get. This fancy fold over method does allow for a cleaner butthole. It's a guarantee that you get most of the left over crap. It is pretty clear when your ass is clean when looking down at a flat, smooth square of toilet paper. If you often received the criticism of smelling, you may want to try this method.

How come we humans are the only animals that wipe our ass? Is it because we are the smartest of all animals? If so, I wish we weren't so smart. Cats and dogs don't wipe their ass and they usually don't smell like manure. I would love to not have to wipe. I would have so much more free time and saved a whole bunch of money on toilet paper. I wonder at what point in our evolutionary chain our ancestors started wiping. This was one big step backwards for mankind. It is now unfortunately too late to get back to those golden days when wiping wasn't necessary.

THE BIOLOGICAL CLOCK

You ever notice you have a bowel movement around the same time each day? Or is that only me? My body is prepared to dump ten minutes after my bowl of cereal in the morning. If my lunch is heavy, it takes an hour before I have to unload. Dinner, for some reason is a 50/50. Half is let go an hour after and the other half is deposited after my snack at night. If for some reason I miss a dump, I am guaranteed a "mile high" the next day. My daily schedule revolves around my shitting. I always give myself enough time in the morning to shit and make sure I have free time to shit in the afternoon. I can't say no to my little but prideful stool specimens. It is bad that they control me but if I disobey them, they always get their revenge.

THE LITTLE THINGS

I have ruined so many pairs of underwear. I leave hash marks (a/k/a skid marks) in all my tighty whities and some of my boxers. It's either from farting or not wiping good. When I don't wipe enough, my ass itches like crazy. So of course I scratch the hell out of it, where I probably ruin my underwear from the rubbing against my dirty ass. Sometimes it comes out in the wash. However, everyone has those pairs where that shit stain is embedded forever. There's nothing you can do about it.

Probably the least heard about phenomenon is the dingleberry. This toilet paper ball, sometimes mixed in with some doody, gets caught in your ass hairs while wiping. It remains there until you shower and wash your ass. These little guys are not that easy to remove. You have to pull them off. Essentially you're pulling the ass hair out in order to get the dingleberry. These guys hurt.

CONSTIPATION

This is not fun. You obviously ate too much rice, stupid. So you find yourself unable to shit. Your whole day is ruined. The desire to shit clouds everything. You try and try but nothing comes out. It's like masturbating but not being able to achieve an orgasm. So eat tons of dairy products, shredded wheat and perhaps a laxative. When it finally comes out, it will be harder than a rock and you'll be absolutely miserable. Expect the worst, and maybe it won't be as bad as you think.

My question about this hold up is where does it go? I have had friends, who I swear have gone 13 days without shitting. Legend has it that one kid went 26 days, holding the overnight camp record. Yes, they were eating and appeared to be healthy. I do not understand how the body can physically do it. Something has to give. There is only so much space in the intestines.

DIARRHEA

Rhea is no fun. I usually get this three times a week. In fact I am surprised when I don't have it. My ass spits out liquid doody like a fire hydrant. It is extremely gross. When I get it, it is multiple times a day. I have gone as many as eleven times in a day but usually average four times when I have it. I cannot plan anything after any meal for I know I will be shitting shortly afterwards. Now, the first few are okay but as the number builds up throughout the day, they start to burn real bad. The pain has brought tears to my eyes.

It seems that I always fall into this mess when I have a big event coming up. It used to be before big basketball games. Quick story. This was my sophomore year in high school. With about two minutes left in the first half of a home basketball game, I felt my stomach churning. I knew what I was in for. I couldn't tell the coach to take me out. That would have been too embarrassing and logical. So I struggled through those longest two minutes of my life. It seemed the game clock kept on stopping. There must have been a hundred whistles blown by the ref during this time. I knew if I made one awkward movement or if I were hit in the stomach, I'd shit on the spot. Now that would have made for a story. So as the time ticked down, I hit a shot at the buzzer and then sprinted to the bathroom for halftime. I missed the coach's halftime speech. I had to go so bad that I didn't bother putting toilet paper on the piss-infested seat. The explosion and relief that followed were definitely in my top three of all time.

Besides sports, my social and academic life have been affected. A few times, I had to send a girl home early from a date due to my runs. It doesn't help me with the ladies when I have to excuse myself to the bathroom three times in an hour. Plus, when I have the squirts I want peace and tranquility. I can't handle any other responsibilities.

I once had such a loose stomach that I couldn't make it through a 45 minute final in high school. I had to run to the bathroom during the middle of it and barely had time to finish the test afterwards.

I probably could limit my diarrhea if I ate better when I had it. But the diet to stop it is almost just as bad. This consists of dry foods such as plain toast, crackers, pretzels and every other dry boring food you could think of. It is a tossup.

These days, with the fat free craze going on, kill me. Yeah, I want to be thin just like everyone else does. So I feel the only way to do this is by eating fat free foods. You can buy almost anything now free from fat. These foods contain all sorts of stuff that rips apart my stomach. For example, the olestra has caused me more pain than getting my wisdom teeth pulled.

I need to talk about my candy, Pepto Bismol. I take this bad boy like it is a daily vitamin. The liquid version is worse than a shot of tequila. The way to go is the chewable kind. At first, these are just as bad. But after taking these for years, I am immune to the taste. Call me sick, but I kind of enjoy them. I think I just realized why Pepto doesn't work for me anymore.

MONTEZUMA'S REVENGE

So during a war of some sort, legend has it that Americans killed a Mexican general or ruler. He left a curse on all Americans known as Montezuma's Revenge. The water would cause horrible pains and bowel movements to all Americans. Well, the curse has worked. Better bring with your bottled water when in Mexico. Our stomachs are not meant to drink their water. Don't even use their ice. Stay away from fruits that can't be peeled. One wrong move could lead to some horrifying effects. We're talking diarrhea for weeks. Quick story. My friend went on a school-sponsored trip to Mexico. While there all the students were told not to drink the water or eat any fruit. The main coordinator of the trip (who warned the students numerous times) disregarded this rule. This poor guy had the shits like none other. Every few minutes he'd be on the can. He shit so much that his toilet overflowed. It overflowed so much that the water leaked out of his room under the door. It flew into the hall way with pieces of shit in it. Not only excruciating pain but eternal embarrassment because all of his students saw it.

Although not in Mexico, I experienced some pain while I was in Fiji. I gulped down their water like it was going out of style. I ate everything in sight. I had to, for it was all-inclusive. So five days later it all hit me. I felt as if there was a baby or alien growing in my stomach. It was the worst pain I have ever come across. I could not sleep or do anything except moan. My girlfriend thought it was gas pains so she gave me permission to fart. Thanks! I ripped some good ones to her surprise but those did nothing except boost my ego. My stomach was going to burst. Even after I shat, my stomach felt full and constantly hurt. I didn't eat for three days, never being hungry. It slowly wore off. A doctor said it may have been a parasite and in some cases they eventually leave your body. Fortunately this sucker left or died.

HEMORRHOIDS

So my freshmen year in college after dropping my kids (my crap) off at the pool, I glance in the toilet and notice some blood. Upon wiping, I see some more. As the day progresses, I notice my underwear is a little wet. I take a look and see more blood. Great. As I shat later that day, it was accompanied by excruciating pain. Each time I tried to contract, it felt as if someone was digging a knife in my ass. So I went to the doctor and let him stick his hand up my ass. Sure enough, it was what I feared most, a hemorrhoid. I was 19-years-old. Hemorrhoids are for parents and grandparents.

I had to go far off campus due to the fear of running into someone I knew and buy some hemorrhoid ointment. Two or three times a day I had to rub this ointment on my asshole. This medicine made me stink. It also ruined all of my boxers.

Most important was the pain that came with this. Every step I took hurt. When I sat down, it hurt. When I shat, the pain was unbearable. If you ever get one, or I should say when you get one, I learned a little trick. When shitting, bring your knees up to your chest and this will ease the pressure on your sensitive asshole.

LACTOSE INTOLERANCE

Why? Why should one not be able to enjoy ice cream and other dairy products? If they do, they'll pay for it greatly. These people are missing an enzyme, lactase, which breaks down lactose. Throughout my life I have had a horrible stomach. I think it runs in the family. So my doctor suggested I take lactaid pills. I tried it for a couple of months. The first month was horrendous. After each meal, in which I took a pill, I suffered incredible stomach pain, followed by an unforgettable dump. I eventually stopped taking these pills yet I still enjoy but am punished later for, consuming dairy products. I think I was misdiagnosed as lactose intolerant. I have learned to accept that I just have a bad stomach. There are actually tests that can reveal whether you are missing the enzyme. I guess my doctor did not believe in testing first. So if you have problems with dairy, ask for a test.

PINWORMS

My mom always yelled at us when we bit our nails saying we would get sick. I can understand why. I had a friend who always bit his nails, who suffered the consequences when he developed pinworms as a kid. He woke up one night due to horrendous butt itching. He then went and took a dump and noticed all these little things swimming around in his stool. Upon aiming a flashlight at his butt and looking in a mirror he saw little worms crawling around. He saw the female worms that left his rectum and were laying eggs around his anus. They were all over including in his bed. Poor kid, cried for days, scared out of his mind. I would be too. He had to get some medicine and it took care of it. You'll never catch him biting his nails now.

THE NAMES

Up until now you have heard numerous names for shit, hopefully some being new to your ears. Anyway here is an almost complete list of synonyms for shit:

crap	shit
doody	poo-poo
cocka	stinky
doody-bomb	doody-ball
bowel movement	dump
hershy squirt	stool
droppings	manure
feces	dookie

SONGS SINCE CHILDHOOD

Farts have been discussed since early age. Here are a few classic slogans that almost everyone knows, that were learned alongside arithmetic in elementary school:

Fe, Fi, Fo, Fum, Joe blew a big one.

Going down the highway, going 64, Johnny blew a big one and knocked me out the door. The wheels couldn't take it, the engine fell apart, all because of Johnny's supersonic fart.

Beans, beans, good for your heart. The more you eat, the more you fart. The more you fart, the better you feel. So eat beans at every meal.

Diarrhea cha-cha-cha, diarrhea cha-cha-cha, some people think it's funny, but it's really dark and runny. Diarrhea cha-cha-cha.

When you're sliding into first and you feel something burst, diarrhea, diarrhea. When you're sliding into second and you feel something beckon, diarrhea, diarrhea. When you're sliding into third and you feel a little turd, diarrhea, diarrhea. When you're sliding into home and you feel a little foam, diarrhea, diarrhea.

These sayings are so embedded within us; they are built into our memory. I probably haven't heard anyone say them since I was a little kid, but they are still very special to me and will always be remembered. If you have any young kids or grandchildren, your popularity will reach new heights by teaching them these.

THE CYCLE OF DUMPING

We are born in this world shitting nothing but yellow, liquid diarrhea. This is only logical in that babies are only nursed at first, with no food. Then as the baby matures and starts being fed food, the stool becomes normal. The baby is given a diaper. Could you believe diapers in the past were not disposable? During this time the child's bathroom life is similar to their life in general, no worries. A baby just goes with the flow with some crying here and there. Personally, I used to shit in the closet during my diaper days. I guess I liked my privacy.

Then comes the toilet training period. This one is the most difficult for the child. The diaper was probably one of their best friends up until this time. Now the child has to learn to sit on a hard seat when he/she feels the urge to poop. The child is so used to shitting whenever he/she has to, that this new restriction, only crapping and pissing in the bathroom, is difficult. Also, it is tough for a child to see the poop come of his/her body. The child is scared to have a part of the body coming out. It is especially difficult when the child poos in a toilet and sees it flushed away. This was a part of them and now they're seeing it vanish. Throughout this training, the child wears training underwear, in case of accidental soiling of the pants. The child in some cases holds back the poo, becoming constipated. During this time, the child suffers stomach pains and smells like crap a lot. When these bricks do come out, they fill up the whole toilet. This fear of dumping usually goes away with age and effective parenting. Finally, the child is potty trained and gets into the routine of shitting.

This period lasts throughout most of the lifespan. Then comes old, old age. Some older people lose control of their bowel movements. They need to wear Depends, which are disposable diapers for adults. I am sort of looking forward to this period when I can kick back and crap in my pants. It's kind of strange or ironic that we start in diapers and end in diapers.

MY IDOL

My life has changed since seeing this event. I have a few goals in life (e.g., bowl a 300 game, hit a golf ball 350 yards in the air) but nothing compares to this new one. One of my best friends can fart over fifty times in a row. I swear I saw it firsthand. He got on his hands and knees, arched his back, made a movement with his ass, farted, did the movement again, and farted, and so on 63 times. I was in complete shock not realizing the drool running down my face. I was salivating like a dog before dinner. How the hell did he do it? He claimed he sucked in air over and over again, through his ass. Absolutely incredible! Brilliant! This guy could do birthday parties or deserves a mention in the Guinness Book of World Records.

So I decided I must learn this technique, but thus far have been unsuccessful. If you want to try it, he arched his back like a cat and flexed his sphincter muscle. Good luck!

GIRLS

When I was 17, I finally realized that girls made poo. Until then I never thought about it. I thought it was strictly a man thing. Well the realization was horrible. So then probably like most men, I made up another image. Girl's shit is completely different than a man's. It smells good and comes out wrapped in a nice box with a bow on it. I know they don't do what we do. It's impossible.

If I am on a date, it's okay, though not good, if I go to the bathroom for 15 minutes. Now if a girl goes by herself and is gone for 15 minutes, that's just wrong. Get rid of her. She's part man. Yes, it's a double standard, but it should be.

I have had nightmares about my girlfriend farting. What if she does? Would I ever be attracted to her again? Would I break up with her? I decided I would give her a 2-week probation. If she did it again, she's gone. No questions asked. Also during this time, there would be no physical touching, partly as a punishment and partly cause I wouldn't want any. Finally, I have only heard about it, but what about the queef? This is the vagina-fart. Is it truly possible? Unfortunately it is possible. A change of pressure causes air to leave the uterus and escape through the closed cervix. This is what causes the noise. Imagine squeezing a balloon's body (the uterus) and the mouth of the balloon is the cervix. The change of pressure and reaction is similar. Sorry to ruin your day. However, this "fart" will not smell. There are no bacteria down here that can cause the same smell in your ass farts.

One of my buddies claims his ex-girlfriend can queef on command. She contracted her tight abdominal muscles, which pushed positive pressure on the uterus. This is difficult but can be done. She performed this disgusting act whenever he asked. I can understand why she is an ex-girlfriend now. She should go work for the circus, that freak.

THE PERFECT INVENTION

Do you want to get rich? Here is the idea of the century. It's the ultimate toilet seat. You make it and I promise I'll buy one. This "seat of all seats" would be as comfortable as a La-Z-Boy. The seat would be a soft cushion. There would be a place for your feet to be elevated, while they were massaged in addition to the massager on the backrest. On your left is the pull out tray, a magazine rack and a radio. To your right is the remote control for your flat-screen TV that is three feet from you, a phone and the refrigerator loaded with beer. You no longer have to worry about missing the last few minutes of the Super Bowl. There is no reason this cannot be developed. Going back to the 2% idea, this definitely would be worth the investment.

You don't like that idea? Here's another. If I had any brains I'd do it myself. I am talking about the fart bag. There is such a thing out, but I need variety. I need all different smells such as the egg fart or the taco fart. This bag when squeezed expands until it bursts, emitting a foul odor. I want a kit that allows me to bag my own fart that I could send to a friend. What a gift! It could turn into like a baseball card collection. Next thing you know kids are trading pop stars, actors, athletes and even the President's farts. What if we could collect a fart from somebody and then reproduce that exact smell? We'd be preserving a special part of somebody and have it to always remember that person even after he/she dies. These fart bags containing the odors from a deceased person, would obviously be more valuable.

FARTS

Of course there is one more area that needs to accompany the topic of dumping. It's comparable to foreplay before sex. It's the fart. This is my favorite. How can one not help but laugh when they hear a fart? I can crack myself up with a loud or stinky one. I think the funniest comedian would be the guy that got up on stage and farted for ten minutes straight. My pet peeve is those guys who get mad when you fart. It is human nature. It's good for you and its funny. Forget those babies who complain. Have a little fun in life. The art of farting is so grand and deserves closer attention. There are numerous types of gassers that should receive universal recognition. Here they are:

1. SBD (silent but deadly). This silent but violent killer is a classic. It can be done anonymously and get reactions from everyone nearby. So much fun. I advise you to move away after expelling it to rule out suspicions. It's best executed when near a crowd.

2. Elevator Fart. Obviously you need more than two people in the elevator. Unless of course you just don't care. This technique is simply marvelous if going up many floors, let's say 15 or more. The shuffling of feet away from the smell is joyful to watch. They have nowhere to go and no clue who was the criminal.

3. Bathtub. I still am amused at making bubbles in the tub. These little stink bubbles do not last too long so a goal of mine is often to try to bite the bubble before it pops. Great for keeping kids busy. Also it makes for a cool science lesson.

4. Shower Fart. Why do farts smell so much worse in a hot shower? It is great. The smell is so potent. The sound is much different as well.

5. Uh-oh Fart. This one takes away all the fun. It is when you anticipate only a fart but get a turd to come out. This is like a premature ejaculation. My father

has thrown away dozens of pairs of underwear throughout his life, having to freeball the rest of the day. He still brags about it.

6. The I-Didn't-Do-It Fart. This one is just cruel. If you are the one out of your friends known to fart, you get this all the time. How do I know? Because I am that guy. If something smells, it must have been me. I get blamed for everything. The worst was during my prom. Everyone was dancing and all of a sudden I noticed a horrible smell. I quickly moved away from it knowing that it would be blamed on me. It was too late, the dance floor cleared off and everyone was laughing and pointing at me. No one would believe me. It is still brought up to this day. I swear I did not do it.

7. The Aged Fart. This is an experimental fart, which was made by farting into a plastic cup and then throwing Saran Wrap around it. The smell only lasts for five days and then dies out.

8. The Dutch Oven. This is quite possibly the best thing since sliced bread. I have never done it to a girl, but I can't wait to. I'll wait until my honeymoon. I have only done it to myself. All you have to do is fart in bed and pull the covers over your head. This preserves the smell leading me to a euphoric, nirvana-like state. I feel bad for my eventual wife.

9. The Rambling Fordooka. This bomb is the textbook fart. It is the roller coaster of farts. It starts quiet and then gets louder and continues to oscillate back and forth between different volumes.

10. The Ground Shaker. This one could rattle the house. It is shocking to hear the decibels of noises your body can produce. This one will definitely wake you up even if you let it out while in a deep sleep.

11. The Squeaker. This is a failed attempt at a SBD usually. In an effort to be polite, you try to be quiet but instead you produce one of these pansy, inexcusable gassers. Not only does everyone notice, but also males look down upon you. And you may be single after your significant other hears this mistaken fart.

12. The Warning Signal. This is like a tornado siren warning of an impending tornado. This fart is crying for a number two. Run immediately to the bathroom.

13. The Egg Fart. Who hasn't heard of this one? It's the classic of classics. The reactions by others to this are priceless. Remember, regardless of how bad a fart smells it always smells good to you if it's your own.

14. The Mary Poppins Fart. Yes, you guessed it. You got to jog a few steps and then jump up clicking your heels while farting at the same time. It is difficult, but phenomenal for those watching. Give it a try.

15. The Running Fart. When you are out for a jog or playing basketball, at often times (or maybe it's just me) a fart develops that has to be let out. It escapes in rhythm with each stride you take. High quality running farts last as many as 30 steps. Never hold it in. Why punish yourself? The only problem is that this guy may be messy. You can't concentrate and don't know exactly what is going to come out. I have ruined many pairs of underwear doing this. Despite being an unfair advantage in sports (been known to add a turbo boost to a run) it is a 10 out of 10 on the difficulty scale.

16. The Classroom Fart. This could be the king of laughs. I have never laughed so hard in my life. Fortunately, I have never been the victim. I have often thought about this and decided that in college if I were ever to fart in class I would have to drop that class. This happened in junior high fortunately not to me. To this day, 13 years later, I still remember the tiny, innocent, quiet girl. I was walking by her when she ripped the biggest fart in the world. I fell to the ground laughing hysterically. Out of all people, it was her, who's name I will not mention. Though I felt bad for her, I could not stop laughing. The few other times someone has ripped ass in class have also brought tears to my eyes. I hoped for it in every class. The poor soul who is caught expelling gas will always be remembered for it.

17. Tushie Burp. This one barely passes as a fart. It's a failed attempt to show off your machoness. It is more like a small burp. If you put your lips together and try to blow out, this is what you get. It is a girlie fart.

ACTIVITIES

Bored? These always-funny pastimes can keep you and others busy. Make a fart tape. It will take a while, but the end product is a magical masterpiece of music. Just keep a tape recorder next to you and each time you have to fart, fart into the microphone. The final tape will be the gift that keeps on giving. It never gets old and your kids will love it. We covered the sound, now let's focus on the picture. Technology has allowed us to do basically anything we want. I use the camera that is built into my cell phone to take pictures of my shits, and then I email them from my phone to my friend's phone or their computer. Just make sure you don't hit the wrong email address when sending it. I do not think your grandmother would appreciate it.

Can people really throw their voice? I don't think so. But people (including me and now you) can throw their own farts. This procedure was named the "buttercup" by my friends and I and its popularity has quickly traveled across the world. Here is how you do it. While farting, take your hand, preferably from your throwing arm and cup it over your asshole. Fart into it, and then close your hand, allowing for some air to remain in the closed hand. Don't make a strong fist. Now quickly take your hand and gently open it under your friend's nose. Or throw it at his face. The best is when you tell your friend to look what's in your hand and then you give him the buttercup. I have peed in my pants laughing so hard after causing some friends to gag from my buttercup.

Don't forget the sacred Whoopee Cushion. This device never gets old. Use it on classmates, teachers, co-workers or whoever. It's always good for a laugh at someone else's expense. And those laughs are the best.

One last activity, which is illegal and I don't suggest doing was made popular in the movies. This is the classic burning shitbag. You shit in a bag, place it on a friend or enemy's doorstep, light it on fire, ring the doorbell, then run and hide behind their bushes. Finally, enjoy the show as they stomp on the burning bag only to see shit pour out of it. If no one answers the door, go put out the fire, dickhead.

WHERE TO FART

Public burping is looked down upon but is permissible. Why is a farter ostracized by society? They are both expelling gas but from different holes. Both can smell. And both are irritating noises, unless they are your own. Why do I have to hold in my gas? Number one, it hurts. Number two, it's fun to fart. Of course if you are with your boys or by yourself, you have the freedom to let 'em rip. With my own family, on behalf of my father's teachings, I would let them rip. My mom would and still does yell at me, but it is worth it. Deep down inside of her I know she likes it and wants to laugh. Who doesn't?

I have yet to purposely fart in front of a girlfriend. This is extremely difficult and needs to be changed. I just hold them in, suffering in pain or I make up some excuse to go outside or upstairs. Once there I get in my squatter's position and fart up a storm. I make sure I get everything out so I don't have to go check on that made up noise again.

If you remember I said I have never *purposely* farted in front of a girl before. This doesn't mean I have never done it. My first one was doing sit-ups in front of my girlfriend. I was on my way up when I ripped a juicy one. Of all my farts, it had to be the rambling fordooka. It nearly knocked her out of her seat. Luckily for me, she laughed about it, teased me for a few days and then dropped it. I, on the other hand, would have gotten rid of her on the spot if the roles were reversed.

So like I said, I have been sacrificing one of nature's greatest gifts up until now when accompanied by my girlfriend. I told my girlfriend, that as soon as "the ring" is on her finger new rules kick in. My mom said my dad never farted until they were married. Like father like son, I will live by the same principle. She can't divorce me for farting. I can't wait to let them rip. Then she'll finally realize I am a true man. I have wanted to give someone besides myself a Dutch oven my whole life.

Looking back, my favorite gasarooskies took place while in college. This took place in the library during finals week. I would go with a few buddies at night to study for our tests. Now imagine, there are rows of individual study booths (carrols). We would all sit next to each other, preferably away from good-looking girls. We'd get into our studies and before you knew it someone would rip one. Each one echoed in the silent library packed with people. I must have ripped a good twenty that night. These weren't your average farts. They were bombs. I felt I was safe, because I was hidden in this booth and was next to two other guys. One of the friends was a pre-med guy so he had complete concentration while studying. He didn't even flinch after any of the gassers, not paying attention to our distractions. If someone walked by or looked at us, my other friend and I would just point at our pre-med friend, passing the blame. During these times, I could not control myself. I laughed non-stop. The pure memory of the fart was enough to make me cry. I laughed so hard that my ribs killed. I had to bite my shirt to stop laughing. This was my sophomore year.

I went back to the library one last time to study for my last final during my senior year. Tears dropped from eyes as I ran into the same friends. I was actually looking forward to studying now. It took me nearly 35 minutes to brew up a fart. When I let it out, it was a tooshie burp, loud enough for only us three to hear. I tried everything possible to get some gas. I tried holding my breath, contracting my butt cheeks, sucking in lots of air. I even went and bought a can of pop, thinking the carbonation would do it. During these two and a half hours, I sadly produced a mere three farts. Despite my shortcoming, my friend let off the M-16 of farts. This puppy echoed for what seemed like minutes. I nearly pissed in my pants from laughing so hard. I went out with a bang. I am sorry to say, these times in the library, filled with fart after fart are among my favorite memories of college.

CONCLUSION

So I hope that you now have a different perspective on shitting. It is gross, but humorous. Why deny its existence? Instead talk about it playfully. If nothing else, I hope this book taught you that you are in fact normal and experience these things just like everyone else. And finally ease up and enjoy everything in life. Remember, 2% or at least 1% of your life is spent on the shitter.

If you enjoyed this book and want additional copies it is available to order at most major book stores or from the following websites:

www.iuniverse.com
www.barnesandnoble.com
www.amazon.com
www.buy.com
www.booksamillion.com
www.walmart.com
www.mediaplay.com

I would like to extend my gratitude to those that helped me. I greatly appreciate your enormous contributions to this work.

0-595-31173-3

13653560R00039

Printed in Great Britain
by Amazon